D0474184

FARMER JOE and the MUSIC SHOW

To Alice Blacker, The Old Crow Medicine Show, and The Hot Bang – T.M.

For Dylan, with special thanks to Liz Johnson and Tim Rose, for their wit and wisdom – G.P.-R.

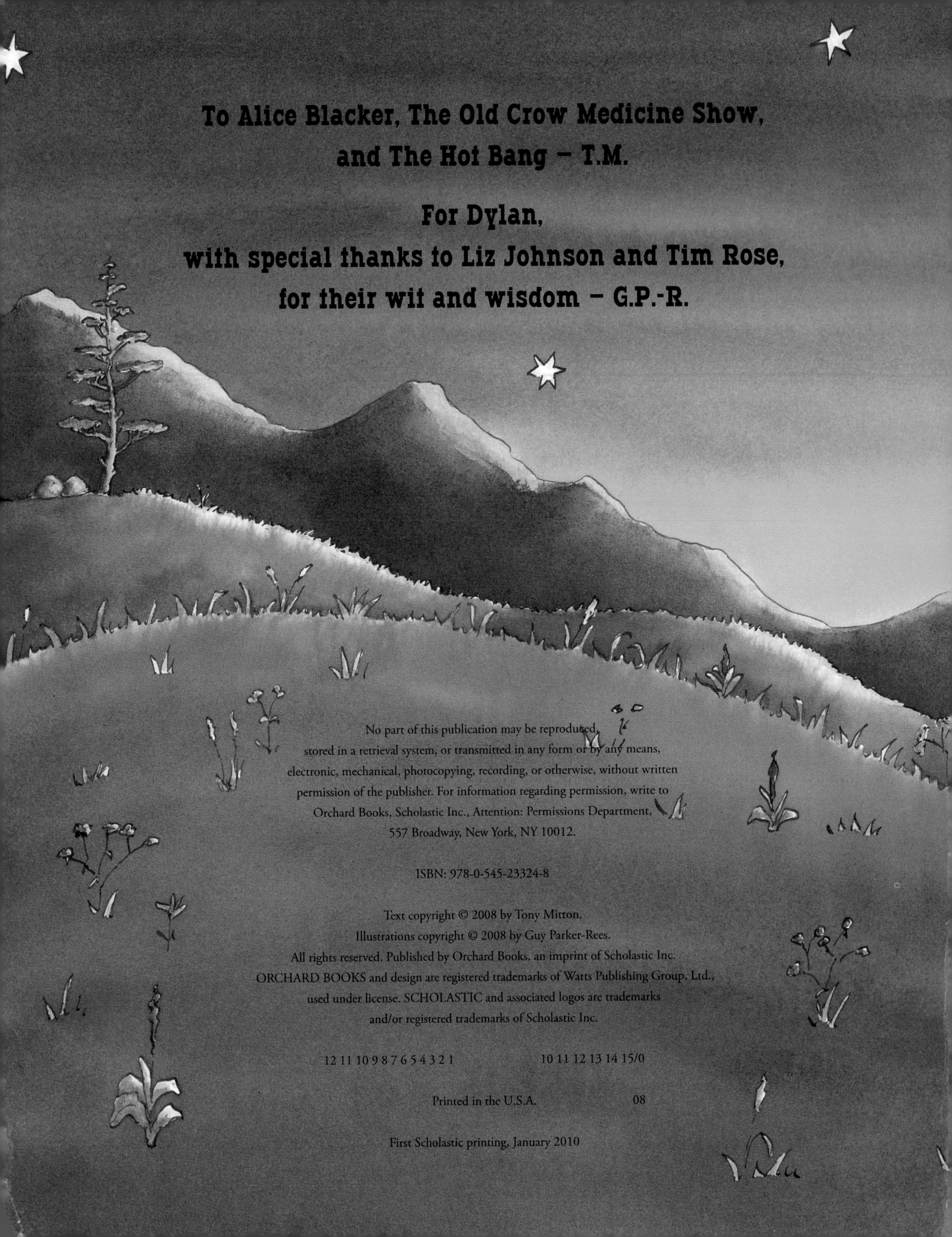

No part of this publication may be reproduced, stored in a retrieval system, or transmitted in any form or by any means, electronic, mechanical, photocopying, recording, or otherwise, without written permission of the publisher. For information regarding permission, write to Orchard Books, Scholastic Inc., Attention: Permissions Department, 557 Broadway, New York, NY 10012.

ISBN: 978-0-545-23324-8

Text copyright © 2008 by Tony Mitton.
Illustrations copyright © 2008 by Guy Parker-Rees.
All rights reserved. Published by Orchard Books, an imprint of Scholastic Inc.
ORCHARD BOOKS and design are registered trademarks of Watts Publishing Group, Ltd., used under license. SCHOLASTIC and associated logos are trademarks and/or registered trademarks of Scholastic Inc.

12 11 10 9 8 7 6 5 4 3 2 1 10 11 12 13 14 15/0

Printed in the U.S.A. 08

First Scholastic printing, January 2010

FARMER JOE and the MUSIC SHOW

By
Tony Mitton

Illustrations by
Guy Parker-Rees

SCHOLASTIC INC.
New York Toronto London Auckland
Sydney Mexico City New Delhi Hong Kong

Down on the farm of Poor Old Joe,
the hens won't lay and the crops won't grow.

The cows won't graze and the pigs won't feed,
and Joe just can't think what they need.

But suddenly Joe has a bright idea:
Music has the power to cheer!

He puts on his hat and yells, "Yee-haw!"

Then he starts to pluck on his old guitar.

pluck-pluck,
plick-plick,
diddle-i-oh

listen to the picking
of Farmer Joe.

The hens start flapping and clucking away...

then they all sit down and start to lay!

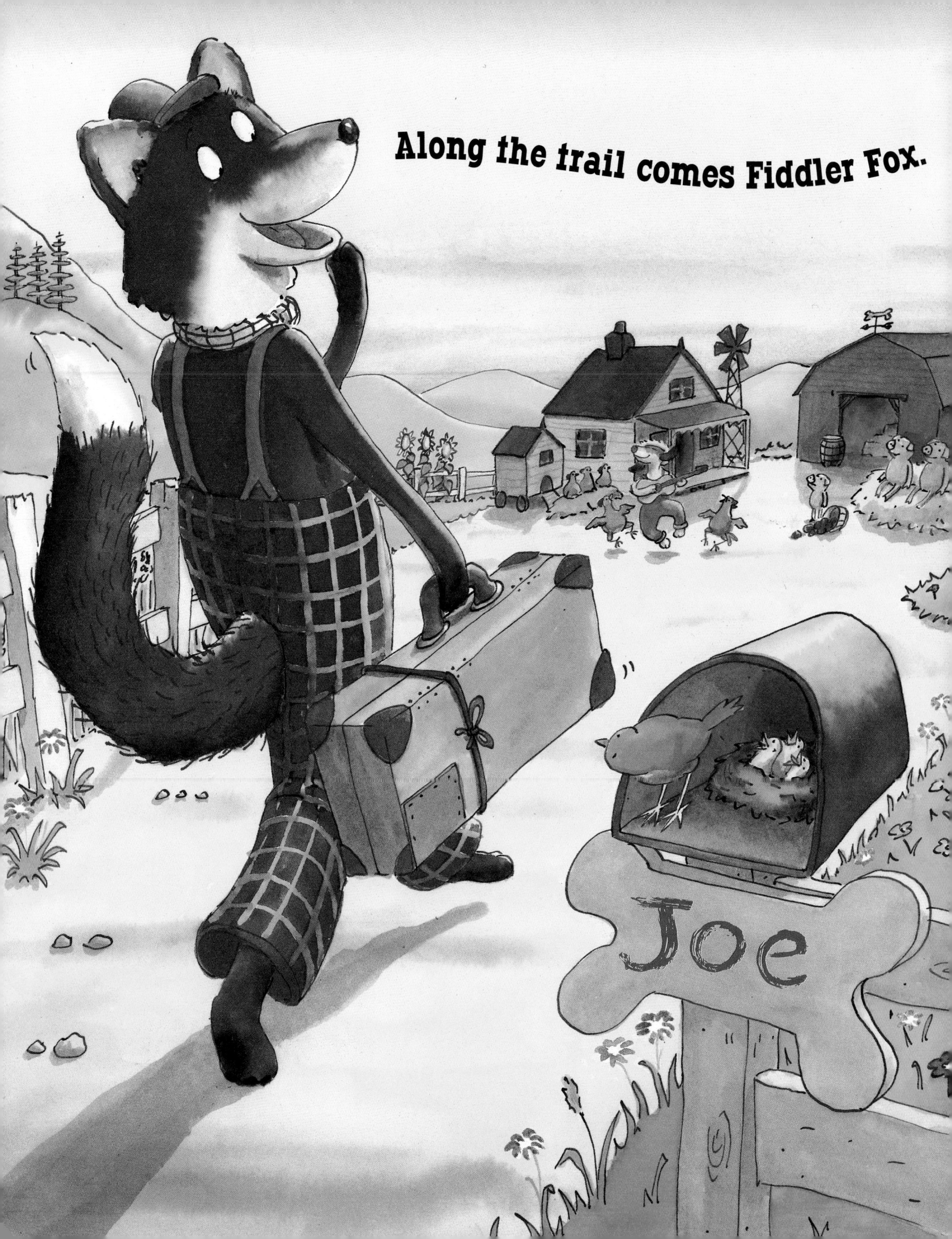

Along the trail comes Fiddler Fox.

He pulls out a fiddle from a battered old box.

He tunes the strings

and he lifts the bow,

then he fiddles to the picking of Farmer Joe.
Pluck-pluck, plick-plick,
yiddle-yiddle-yiddle,
Joe on guitar and Fox on the fiddle,

playing it nifty, playing it neat,
till the pigs start dancing to the music's beat.

Out of a burrow pop two big ears.
Rabbit just loves
that stuff she hears.

She hops from her hole and starts to play
on a concertina, right away!

Concertina, wheee-hee-hah,
skiddly fiddle and old guitar.
The crops like the music. Me-oh-my!
Look at them stretching up to the sky!

Now, what's that rumbling, grumbling sound?
Something **big** is stumbling round.

Soon we'll see it face to face . . .

Bear's bass booms with a deep, low thrum.

The bass makes a buzz and the day looks sunny . . .
so out come the bees humming,
"Let's make honey!"

Joe's on guitar with Fox on the fiddle,
Rabbit's concertina fits in the middle,

the bees go buzz as they hum around,
and Bear's bass booms as he stomps the ground.

Bull wakes up. What's this he hears?
"Herd!" he bellows.
"Now, lift your ears!"

The cows start mooing as the music plays,
then they click their hooves as they bend to graze.

The creatures caper – look at them go –
to the thrill of the hillbilly music show.

They jump and jive.
They leap and bound.
They love the rhythm of the country sound.

But now it's hot, and the sun rides high,
and the heat beats down from the big, blue sky.

What'll they do now?
What do you think?
Sprawl in the shade with a nice, cool drink.

And Farmer Joe can smile and strum,
and say, "Just let those
sweet tunes come. . .

"No need to mope and moan around.
We've found the power of music's sound.
If the pigs won't feed
and the hens won't lay...

"... I'll get my little old band to play!"

He thanks his friends
for the good they've done.
Then they play some more now,
just for fun.

So down on the farm of Clever Old Joe,
the hens all lay and the crops all grow.
The cows all graze and the pigs all feed,
and Joe knows just the thing they need.